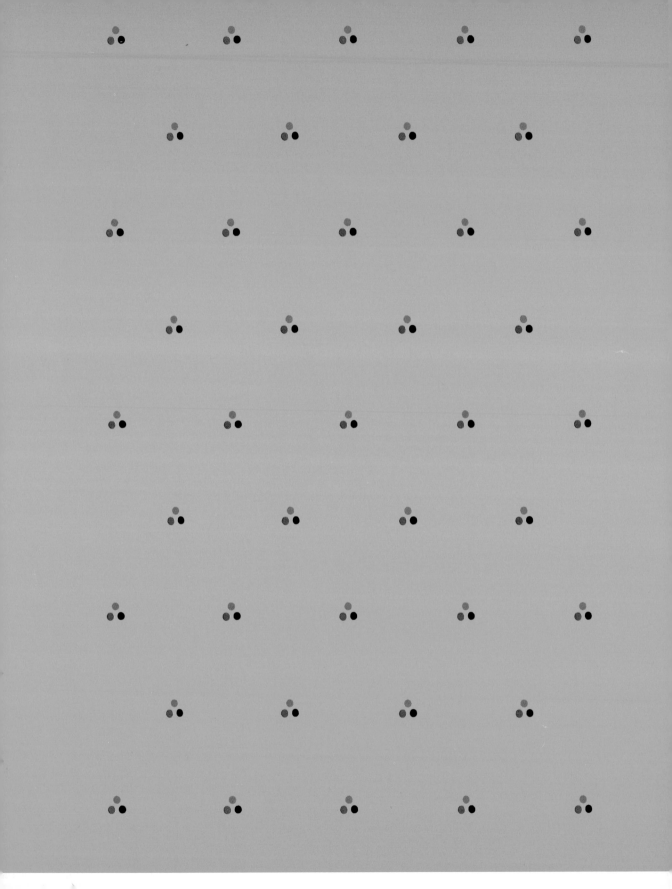

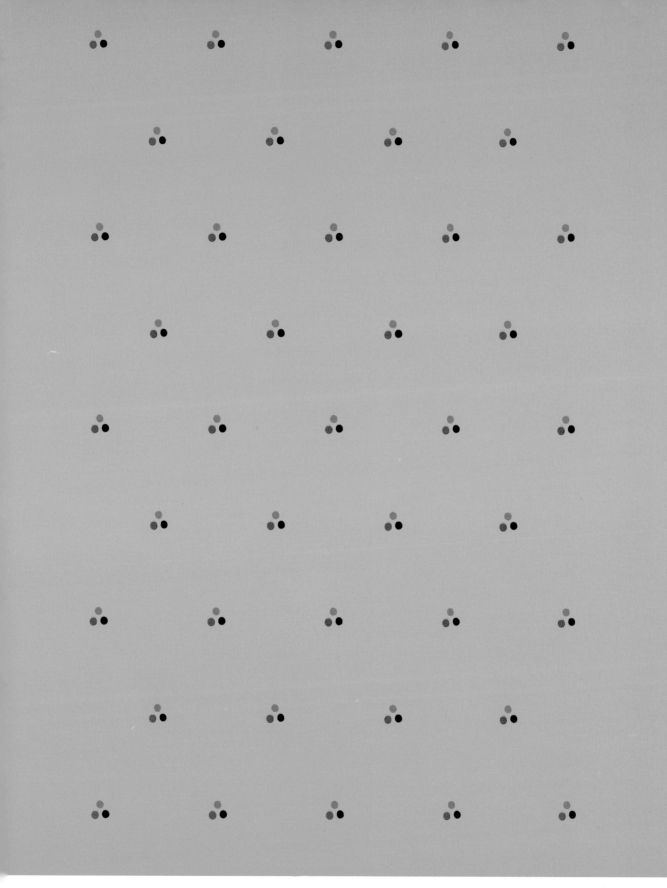

Imani's Gift at Kwanzaa

by Denise Burden-Patmon

Illustrated by
Floyd Cooper

MULTICULTURAL CELEBRATIONS

MODERN CURRICULUM PRESS

Multicultural Celebrations was created under the auspices of

The Children's Museum, Boston.
Leslie Swartz, Director of Teacher Services,
organized and directed this project with
funding from The Hitachi Foundation.

Design: Gary Fujiwara
Photographs: *2, 12,* The Children's Museum;
6, Pamela Johnson Meyer; *21,* Greater Cleveland
Kwanzaa Alliance.

MODERN CURRICULUM PRESS, INC.
13900 Prospect Road
Cleveland, Ohio 44136

ISBN 0-8136-2243-3 (soft cover)   0-8136-2244-1 (hard cover)

2 3 4 5 6 7 8 9 10   95 94 93 92

Simon & Schuster   A Paramount Communications Company

Grandmother braided Imani's hair. Imani loved the
braiding times. They were special times she and
M'dear shared. They were times of talking and
times of listening.

"Oh M'dear," said Imani. "Today is my favorite day of *Kwanzaa*. Tonight will be our feast! And I will be the one to light the candles and tell what *Kuumba* means to me."

M'dear brushed a section of Imani's soft, curly hair. Then she began to make individual braids. She wove small beads into each braid. The beads were red, black, and green—the colors of *Kwanzaa*. She sang softly.

With the red, remember the hard work that has been;
With the black, show the beauty that is you;
With the green, show faith in the plenty that will be.

2

"*Kuumba* is my favorite day of *Kwanzaa* too, Imani," she said. "*Kuumba*—creativity—reminds us of the beautiful things our people make."

"There sure is a lot of *Kuumba* around here today, M'dear. You are making something beautiful when you braid my hair—right?"

Grandmother laughed. "Right, my Imani. I'm making something very beautiful. Now let me finish what I was saying."

"*Kwanzaa* is an African word that means *first*," M'dear continued. "For hundreds of years, our ancestors in Africa celebrated the harvest of the first crops. Now *Kwanzaa* names a special holiday for African Americans.

"In December, during the seven days of *Kwanzaa*, our families and friends come together," she explained. "We sit and eat and talk together. We remember the good and important things that have taken place during the past year. We tell about the work we must do to make even better things happen. We give thanks for each other. We give special thanks for our children—the *watoto*."

6

"There is one *watoto* I do not give thanks for,
M'dear. Will *you-know-who* come tonight, M'dear?
Did Mama invite Enna and Mrs. Johnson?" asked
Imani in an unhappy voice.

"Imani, you know you have a real place in this
family. Your parents have shown their love for you
by the proud name they gave you. Can't you share
some of that love with Enna?"

"M'dear, Enna teases me about my name.
She makes fun of lots of other things, too. She says
mean things."

Imani's cheeks became wet with tears. M'dear
drew her close.

"It's hard to show love when you haven't seen very much. Enna hasn't. She has had no one to believe in her. She has had no one to tell her who she is and where she came from.

"Enna is part of the Johnson family now—and a part of our neighborhood. Of course she will be coming to our dinner tonight. And it's up to us to help her know the joy and beauty of what we're celebrating."

There was a thinking silence.

"What is the first idea of *Kwanzaa*, Imani?" M'dear asked softly.

"We say '*Umoja*.' It means *unity*—coming together," Imani answered in a soft voice.

"Then if you know what unity is, my Imani, you will want to help Enna—right?"

Imani did not answer.

The day went quickly. Wonderful smells filled the house. Ummmmmmmm! Imani could smell Mama's delicious pies.

Imani worked with her family to get ready for their dinner. While they moved furniture, her brother Haki played tapes of his favorite African music. Her sister Aretha hummed along as she cleaned. Everyone in the house was full of joy and excitement.

Imani helped Uncle Maceo prepare the *mkeka* for the table. She placed the ears of corn on the straw mat. She made sure there was one ear of corn for each child—including Enna.

Next, Imani laid out the candles. "Uncle Maceo, remember that I'll be the one to light the six candles tonight—one for each day of *Kwanzaa* so far."

"Why, who else would be able to do it, Miss Imani?" teased her uncle. "You are the one with the special name."

As she worked, Imani thought and thought about what her grandmother had said. By afternoon she had made up her mind. She went to her room and worked by herself.

Evening came and it was time to light the candles. M'dear called to Imani to come and join them.

"*Habari gani*, Enna," Imani said in greeting. But Enna did not know how to answer. This was Enna's first *Kwanzaa*.

"It's *Kwanzaa*, Enna. During *Kwanzaa* we answer the greeting with the idea of the day. Today's answer is '*Kuumba*'."

Enna tried the word softly, saying, *"Kuumba."*

Imani caught Enna's hand in her own. "They're waiting for us to begin the *Karamu,* but come to my room for just a minute. I have something to give you."

"This is a gift." Enna looked at Imani, surprised. "You have a gift—for me?"

"It's a *zawadi*—a *Kwanzaa* gift. It shows *Kuumba*— something I made that is special. Open it!"

Enna tore open the paper. She looked down at the words and pictures Imani had carefully formed. It was beautiful writing, but she did not understand what the words meant.

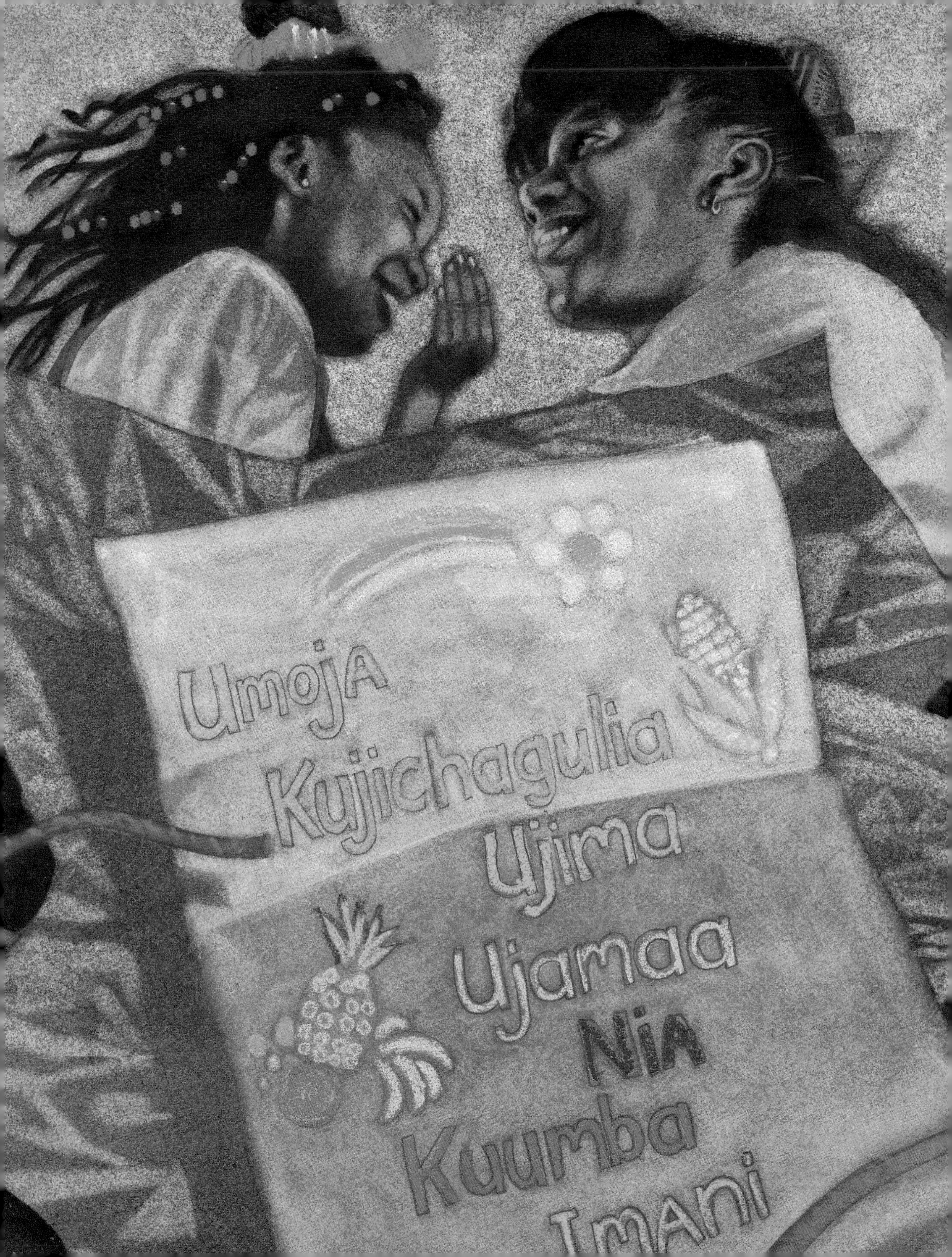

Umoja
Kujichagulia
Ujima
Ujamaa
Nia
Kuumba
Imani

"Those are the *Nguzo Saba* —the seven ideas of *Kwanzaa*," Imani explained. "I don't know about all of them. If you want, together we can ask M'dear to tell us about each one."

"Oh yes, I'd like that," said Enna with a shy smile.

"And Enna—you'll never guess what day it will be tomorrow," Imani said.

"Well, it's just Sunday, isn't it?" asked Enna.

"No, not really. It will be the seventh day of *Kwanzaa*—the day of *IMANI!*" Imani said and began to giggle.

After a moment, Enna giggled with her.

Glossary

(These words come from the African language called *Swahili*.)

Habari gani (hah-BAH-ree GAH-nee) a greeting that means "What's the news?"

Karamu (kah-RAH-moo) Kwanzaa feast

Kwanzaa (KWAHN-zah) first, or first fruits; also names an African-American celebration that takes place the last week in December

M'dear (mah-DIR) nickname for grandmother indicating warmth and affection

mkeka (mah-KAY-kah) a straw mat used in the Kwanzaa celebration

Nguzo Saba (nah-GOO-zoo SAH-bah) the seven principles of the Kwanzaa celebration that guide African Americans in their lives. The principles are:

> **Umoja** (oo-MOH-jah) unity;
>
> **Kujichagulia** (koo-jee-cha-goo-LEE-uh) control of your own life;
>
> **Ujima** (oo-jee-MAH) working together and responsibility;
>
> **Ujamaa** (oo-jah-MAH) sharing money and profits;
>
> **Nia** (NEE-ah) having a purpose or reason;
>
> **Kuumba** (koo-UM-bah) being creative;
>
> **Imani** (ee-MAH-nee) having faith.

watoto (wah-TOO-too) children

zawadi (zah-WAH-dee) a gift given during Kwanzaa

About the Author

A former public school teacher, **Denise Burden-Patmon** teaches in the English Department and the Education Department at Wheelock College in Boston. She has written widely on multicultural education, curriculum development, and teaching writing to children. This book is dedicated to her beloved mother, Mamie Jarrell Burden, who taught her to be kind, gentle, and to celebrate her African-American roots.

About the Illustrator

Floyd Cooper was born and raised in Tulsa, Oklahoma. He received a degree in fine arts from the University of Oklahoma and apprenticed under artist Mark English. After working for a greeting card company, Mr. Cooper moved to New York City to pursue a career as an illustrator of books for young people. His first book, *Grandpa's Face* (by Eloise Greenfield; Philomel, 1988) was named an American Library Association Notable Book for Children.

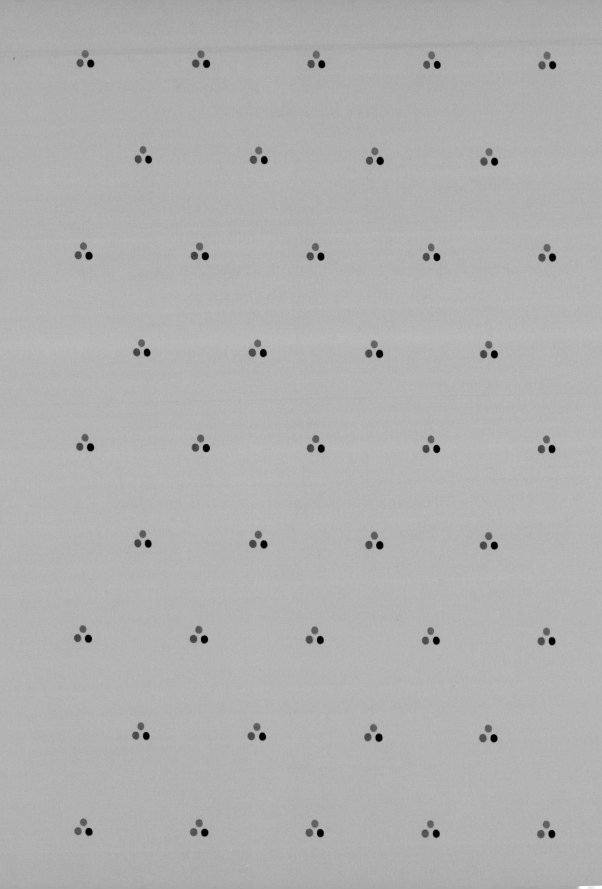

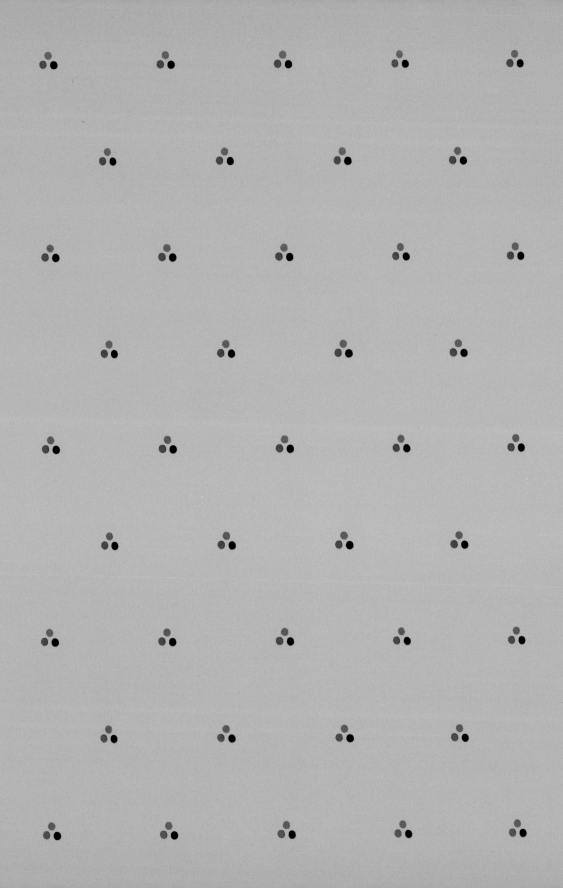